THE RACCOONS

THE RACCOONS

BRIONY ERIN MIKELL

Briony Erin Mikell
The Raccoons

Published by Spines
ISBN 979-8-89691-871-4

CONTENTS

1. Earth's Rebirth   1
2. The Raccoon That Went Against The Grain   5
3. The New Neighbor   9
4. Change in Perspective   17
5. The Roar Heard Around The Block   23
6. Eye of The Tiger   27
7. Animals Make The World Go Round   33

CHAPTER 1

EARTH'S REBIRTH

In the furthest future of Earth's time, humans were forced to live with animals and lose their place as the top beast. Humans depended on technology, and their activities changed the animals' chemistry. New tech for advanced AI was created to improve function and performance, and everyone used it. However, one robot went rogue, and it caused a chain reaction by exposing its biofuel to fossil fuel, releasing a toxin, a virus. It spread fast, destroying many plantations. Some places became mucky swamps with many blacker waste pools than oil, smelling even worse than landfills. The only way the virus reached the rest of the world was by boat and air travel by planes, and humans were the carriers until the virus died on its own.

By the time the virus killed itself, it slowly evolved all the animals except most farm animals, bugs, and sea life. They could walk and talk like humans. The animals even ran the world like humans once did. They were also large, and many were taller than humans. Farm animals save for horses, and sheep remained the same, raised to provide food. The sheep, horses, and other equine creatures evolved a bit later. The virus couldn't affect any water creatures, for it died on water contact.

The animals began to outnumber humans and the billions of towns and cities humans used to have turned into seven large cities, and of course, they were all run by animals. Because the animals were in control, the Earth restored itself and was healthy again. Robots were limited, and the new ones that caused the spread of the toxin were all scraped. Specific resources and fuels were banned since retrieving them meant destroying the Earth. The humans didn't mind, for they knew they were the ones who caused the Earth to become sick.

One of the seven cities went by the name Beast Dump, which was once the City of Chicago and was the least beautiful in more ways than one. The city reverted to its swamp state, and many of the buildings surrounding the lake were underwater, which enhanced the crowding issue.

The other towns were Leon Sand, Forest Dream, Dragon Bamboo, Flying Frost, Isle Breeze, and Sea Base.

In Beast Dump, the animals lived together but not harmoniously. Certain animals that made up the lower class were mistreated. One of those animals was the raccoon. They were called "Rats," "Thieves," and "Garbage," mainly because they ate the humans' trash back when humans ran the world. However, the raccoons were exceedingly kind and intelligent.

The jobs they were "allowed" were keeping the city clean and helping everyone find homes and jobs, but they were paid little. They were mistreated along with the rats, wolves, bats, hyenas, and snakes. By day, the raccoons did their jobs but gave extra help to the other mistreated animals by night. They gave poor wolf and hyena families meat and offered rats and snakes their basements to sleep for the night, and the rats and snakes switched with the bats when the day returned. No one knew why the raccoons did this, and no one asked them.

The raccoons knew that Beast Dump's conditions weren't suitable, but they made the best of it and taught the other mistreated animals to do the same. Humans loved the raccoons and would joke about them being related to "Rocket" from "Marvel's Guardians of the Galaxy." Since many worked as architects, they made rooms by building new homes to house as many homeless animals as possible. Many wished to do more, be more.

Even though humans were now few, they were vocal about the treatment of individual animals. They claimed that animals were cruel to each other, which reminded them of how they used to treat each other and even the animals. However, the animals ignored the humans, calling them hypocrites. The humans could see and understand why the animals wouldn't listen to how they treated each other.

Humans didn't even expect the animals to trust them after what they did. They bred and domesticated many animals, abused them in many ways, some too cruel to mention, and were unfortunate and humiliated. The humans agreed to help the animals when they asked for it. They understood that they should have respected nature enough not to change it and let it heal itself. That also means letting the animals work their differences out themselves.

The raccoons, rats, bats, snakes, hyenas, and wolves made up the Lower class of Beast Dump, while the herbivores and omnivores were Middle class, and the carnivores were Upper class. The divide was very noticeable, and watching it unfold had some humans who didn't want to wait for change to come on their own to help the lower class to the best of their ability. However, they knew that only an upper-class predator who saw things differently would change how the raccoons and other lower-class creatures were treated.

CHAPTER 2

THE RACCOON THAT WENT AGAINST THE GRAIN

Many raccoons wished to do and be more, but one stood out by doing more than just hope. There was a raccoon who went by the name of AJ Walker. He was an artist, and his studio apartment was filled with sketches, paintings, and sculptures. However, he worked as a landscaper. He loved the job but hated the treatment he was given. All he wanted was for people to appreciate his craft and use of color, but no one tried. Only his neighbors, raccoons and the other lower-class beasts loved this craft, and when they had a block party, they turned it into an art show.

AJ's neighbors were the reason he continued his craft. However, he could sense they were mainly interested because they used his art to support their dreams and businesses, but when he needed comfort, they were always busy. He felt used and alone and wished he had one other person who honestly had his back beside himself. Even his parents didn't show support, and it was like that since he was young. They didn't understand his interest in his craft, so he taught and learned about it independently. When he asked what people thought about his work, no one showed infusionism as they would with other things. He became very selective with who he hung around because of it. He was lonely at times, but he refused to try to work with animals that didn't see what they were doing and weren't willing to change.

His only comfort was his three daughters, Christie, Joan, and Lily. Christie was twelve and Autistic, and she shared the same passion for art as AJ and made it a point to learn all from him. Joan was eight, and Lily was four. To AJ, they were his world and maybe the only girls that genuinely got him, save for perhaps their mother when she was alive.

AJ didn't want to think that it was best to be alone. He wanted to believe that other animals besides raccoons, rats, snakes, bats, wolves, and hyenas care and want things to change. His mom would tell him he wished and dreamed of something that would never exist. She would say, "Only a raccoon can understand a raccoon. That will never change. Don't seek help outside our species."

AJ still thinks there should be at least a few animals, not raccoons, who care enough to notice the injustice and want to do different, be different. He didn't want to think his mother was right. He was determined to teach his daughters to be careful about whom to trust and to believe in the nature any animal shows them, no matter what they are

taught and told. That means they can be friends with any beast that shows kindness despite differences. His heart was warm when they told him they had befriended a young fox pup. He hopes that the friendship sticks and there will be more to come. He even dared to wish he could have a friend that is not a raccoon, someone different. Having a friend, in general, would be helpful, in AJ's opinion. He did try to find a friend on his block, but he's a very giving creature, and any attempt to form any friendship always felt one-sided. His only friend was his girls' mother. Her name was Marsha.

Marsha had been his friend since they were little, and they did everything together growing up. She was the one that got him into photography and art. Many of his works' subjects were her, and Marsha didn't mind being his muse. Then Marsha was poisoned a year after she had Lily. They had food delivered, and someone put rat poisoning in Marsha's food. Sheep was running the restaurant. Though the sheep were imprisoned and the restaurant was demolished, AJ was mostly sad, missing Marsha.

To AJ, everything seems black and grey. It was rare for him to see color on good days. There were days he would paint, and he only used the colors grey, black, and blue, reflecting that he was thinking of Marsha. There were pots full of mini roses that sat outside the apartment windowsills, which Marsha always loved and tended to. AJ let them grow wild and unkempt after she passed until Christie took over taking care of them. Marsha's dream was to start a garden on the roof to make the block greener and full of life. With her gone, it may never happen.

AJ's daughters tried their best to cheer him up, and they usually do, most of the time. He would smile every time Christie created a picture, when Joan would dance, or when Lily was silly and bubbly, but they would remind him of their mother, and a little of that sadness dampened his smile. They all reminded him of Marsha in their own way and missed their mother. Christie and Joan remembered her well, but Lily had the least number of memories of her. Lily would sometimes ask about her, and AJ would tell her. He was sad, and she heard it in his voice, but she would hug him to comfort him. The whole neighborhood missed Marsha, and the entire block believed it was time for a change for everyone, especially AJ and his daughters.

CHAPTER 3
THE NEW NEIGHBOR

One day, an Autistic tiger named Jasmine Rose moved into Beast Dump. She was shy, and the world was loud and strange to her. Though she didn't finish school, she wanted to be a writer, and she came to the city to try to get her writing published. She started her floral business to make money in the meantime. She came from Dragon Bamboo, a town in the land once called China. Everyone in her family wanted her to be a doctor since everyone in her family was a doctor. They were known and praised for tending animals and humans. However, Jasmine's calling was writing, which is why she left.

Jasmine loved flowers almost as much as writing, and she started a garden and greenhouse on the roof of the apartment building she moved into. She planted seeds but also potted flowers. When she opened a website for her flower business, orders flooded in. Working in her garden gave her peace and a moment to think about ideas for books to write.

Jasmine pitched the first drafts of stories she wrote, but they were all denied for the moment. While her flower business kept her content, she contacted several publishing companies and kept being turned down. One day, she came to one that told her to present new writing material in 6 months, and if they liked it, it would be published as a book. Jasmine wasn't happy, but she was determined to write something meaningful.

When she returned to her apartment, she heard voices that didn't sound pleasant. Jasmine went to see what was happening and saw a raccoon cowering, towered over by a badger and a hawk.

"Dirty raccoon" was one of the things she heard them say.

The hawk struck the raccoon again with his talons, and the raccoon received a scratch near his left eye.

"Hey, pick on someone your own size! Don't you see he's not fighting back?" Jasmine spoke up.

The badger turned sharply at her with a hiss, but the hawk flew off in fright. "Why do you care about what I do to this trash? A tiger shouldn't even be here." The badger stated challengingly.

"I live here, which makes that raccoon my neighbor, and I don't like what you are doing to him," Jasmine said firmly. After 30 seconds of silence, the badger backed off.

While he left, he said, "I advise you to leave this part of Beast Dump. Raccoons are not to be trusted. They'll rob you blind."

Once the badger was entirely out of sight, Jasmine helped the raccoon to his feet.

"Who was that?" Jasmine asked with an annoyed tone.

The raccoon snorted and shook its head, "Oh, that's just JoJo. He thinks he runs the block since he's the only badger here. The hawk was his buddy, Randall. He's a tail licker, if you ask me".

Jasmine then invited the raccoon for tea. She watched him amusingly as he glared all around her home and struggled to keep from laughing when she heard him comment in amazement at the items in her home. 'How could she afford this?' was the main thing he asked himself. Jasmine had vases, paintings, bowls, and jade sculptures from many human cultures in China. There were even scrolls that had Chinese writing that read words like "Peace," "Honor," "Respect," and "Loyalty." Once the tea was brewed and both animals sat across each other in the living room, Jasmine decided to start the introductions. "So, raccoon, what's your name?" Jasmine asked.

The raccoon hesitated initially, but he could sense that she wasn't like the other animals he usually ran into. "The name's AJ. What's yours?".

"Jasmine."

AJ looked the tiger up and down and smiled. "I do remember seeing you once when you first moved here. JoJo, though I hate to admit it, does have a point. There are nicer places to live than here, so why here?"

Jasmine laughed. "It's not because I can't afford a luxurious place. I just don't want to. I want to work my own way up here", Jasmine explained.

"So, your parents have money?" AJ asked, confused.

"Yes, but I only accepted enough to get to the city, buy a place to stay, food, internet, and rent for six months. If they had their way, I would be in a house in the suburbs or still be home with them." They started talking, sharing their stories, while Jasmine tended to AJ's scratches. What AJ told Jasmine alarmed her. In Dragon Bamboo, all animals are respected like family, but some are mistreated in Beast Dump.

Jasmine decided to interview this raccoon and any raccoon, wolf, rat, bat, snake, or hyena willing to share. Jasmine even spoke to humans, asking how they treated animals and each other.

While interviewing AJ, Jasmine learned about him and his three girls: Christie, Joan, and Lily. She was even invited into the house where she met the girls for the first time. Lily warmed up to Jasmine right away. While Joan was skeptical and distant at first, Christie bonded with Jasmine the most, and Christie was inspired to be a writer and artist. Jasmine even learned that Christie was bullied at school, and the teachers believed she was lazy. Jasmine had her tell AJ, and together, they straighten things out. The teachers were now understanding and helped Christie, but the bullies were meaner. Jasmine told Christie to speak to the teachers and tell them what was happening. Jasmine even gave her a gift. It was a sack with twelve Trouble Dolls.

"You just have to share your problem with a doll and place it in the sack. The doll will stay in there until the problem is solved. However, you only have twelve, so you can only have twelve problems a day, ok?" Jasmine told Christie. Jasmine also noticed AJ's unkept home and taught his girls to clean up, which helped AJ greatly. AJ explained that his mate always kept their house clean. AJ was grateful that his girls had someone to look up to, even though she was of a different species. He could tell that they trusted her and saw her as a mother, and he had to explain that he and Jasmine were only friends when Lily asked if he was going to marry her. They were disappointed, but they under-stood. They also understood that different types of animals couldn't breed due to genetic compatibility.

Jasmine even began conducting interviews for her book in her garden. Many loved her garden and would offer to help work on it with her. The work went faster, and she was convinced to have a vegetable garden. Jasmine was happy to bring animals and humans together in her garden and hoped she could do the same with her book. Jasmine convinced the publishing company to extend the time she spent presenting her book idea, which they granted.

Jasmine was happy to have AJ as a friend but also missed her old friends at home. She began a video chat and caught up with them, and they were excited to meet AJ and his girls. Jasmine's friends were Li, the raccoon, Sue, the white tiger, and Lan, the monkey, and they became fast friends with AJ. They were even excited that Jasmine was working on a book to show the different treatments of animals in Beast Dump.

One particular day, Jasmine and AJ talked with Li, and Li said, "AJ, I'm glad Jasmine has you as a friend. One raccoon has to keep an eye on her."

Jasmine blushed, embarrassed, and AJ smiled as he replied, "She's been delightful to my girls and me. I'm grateful she came here."

"Has she met your family? You should let me know when you do so I can say 'Hello.'" Li asked.

AJ's eyes widen in alarm. "You two do NOT want to meet my family, especially my mom."

"Why not?" Li and Jasmine asked together.

AJ sighed and replied, "She thinks that no animal is capable of change, and so she drilled this thought in the entire family's head not to trust any other animal besides raccoons."

Li made a strange face on Jasmine's phone screen. "I'm not too worried. When she sees Jasmine, she'll come around. I honestly believe that."

"I'm not sure, but we'll see," AJ stated.

Jasmine understood and shared his worries. If his mother is anything like her parents, she will give her son a challenging time befriending a tiger. At first, Jasmine did consider breaking ties but realized it wouldn't be fair to AJ and his girls, especially since she would be taking the choice away from them. Jasmine had to believe that AJ could somehow get through to his family.

CHAPTER 4

CHANGE IN PERSPECTIVE

One day, AJ's family came to visit. It was unannounced, but AJ was happy to see them and introduced them to Jasmine. It didn't take long for them to warm up to her. They were excited about Jasmine's book and offered to help and be a part of it. Only AJ's mother gave Jasmine the cold shoulder and refused to be part of the conversation. AJ's parents ventured into a spare room and argued quietly. Christie, Joan, and Lily expressed concern and confusion about their grandmother's behavior toward their dad.

"Your Grandma loves you. Don't ever doubt that. She just wants what's best for the family, but she just doesn't trust other animals besides our own.", AJ explained.

Jasmine overheard and thought about her family. Their closest friends were raccoons, and there was no discrimination. What would they think of AJ's mother if they found out what she thought of her? AJ's parents soon returned from the spare room and confronted AJ and Jasmine. She hopes that her raccoon friend, Li, is right about AJ's Mother coming around and getting to know her.

"Can you send your girls to their rooms? I would like to speak with you and your 'friend.'" AJ's mom requested.

"My girls are fine where they are. What do you wish to tell us?" AJ stated firmly.

After a pause, AJ's mom said, "It is inappropriate to have a tiger here, especially around our kids." She turns to Jasmine. "Why are you even in this neighborhood? What do you want from my son?"

Jasmine restrains from growling and replies, "I want nothing but friendship with all fellow beasts. I assure you, Mrs. Walker, I mean no harm or ill will toward AJ and his girls."

"Ha, a likely story. AJ doesn't need you, and I don't want you near my granddaughters. You're from Dragon Bamboo, right? Return there because all you tigers are the same, devourers to all that moves." AJ's mom snorted.

"Like our stripes, every tiger is different. Where I come from, raccoons and tigers are friends. I want that for Beast Dump and AJ, and I am working on a book to do that." Jasmine said calmly.

"You are exploiting my son for personal gain, and I won't stand for it. Leave his apartment!"

"Grandma, why are you being mean? Jasmine has done nothing wrong." Christie said, "She's nice to us and Dad, and she's helped me with problems at school."

AJ's mother glared a Christie with wide eyes and looked back at Jasmine with a snarl.

"You even brainwashed my Granddaughters. You leave now!" AJ's mom shouted.

Everyone grew quiet then, sensing the tension. AJ walked around his girls and Jasmine and was only an inch away from his mother.

"You can leave if Jasmine makes you uncomfortable. She is unlike the other beasts, and you have no right to tell me who I can be friends with. Jasmine saved me from JoJo the first few days she was here. She's humble, kind, and smart enough not to be what we claim all tigers are. She wants nothing from me, is sweet to my girls, and wants to better our situation. You only want to believe what you want to see, but everyone in our family shouldn't only go off what you say. If you can't see that, then you leave. You don't even have to come back, but that will mean you won't see your granddaughters." He hissed.

AJ's mother's eyes widened in shock at her son's words, and she quickly looked around to see the family glare back with disapproval and alarm.

"Is that how you all feel?" she asked.

Everyone nodded. AJ's mom glared at her mate. "Are you just going stand there and let our son talk to me like that?" she demanded.

AJ's father, Mr. Walker, looked at his mate and looked at AJ with a smile as he placed a paw on his shoulder.

"My son is his own raccoon, and I'm very proud. Once upon a time, 'Only a raccoon understands a raccoon' worked for us, but I see no malice in Jasmine. Nature always changes. That's what makes it natural, and I think we can all learn from AJ, his daughters, and Jasmine here."

He looked at Jasmine and declared, "Welcome to the family, Jasmine. Welcome"

"Welcome, Jasmine. Welcome!" said the rest of the family.

AJ's mom said nothing else, defeated by the sight of the family befriending a tiger. After that visit, AJ's mother stopped speaking to him. However, the rest of the family did. They shared stories with Jasmine for her to add to her book. After a while, AJ's mother came around and tried to get to know Jasmine. She shared stories for the book and met Jasmine's friends, Lan, Sue, and Li. Through the stories, Jasmine understood why Mrs. Walker wasn't so trusting with other animals, and soon, they became close, which made Jasmine wish she were intimate with her parents and could talk and understand each other.

Mrs. Walker was now more like a mother to Jasmine. There were times AJ felt like his mother was doing too much. One time, Jasmine was sick with a severe cold and couldn't get out of bed because her body ached, so she couldn't sell her flowers or work on her book. She told AJ, and he told his mother; however, his mother came to Jasmine's apartment before he did. It made Jasmine smile, hearing AJ and Mrs. Walker fuss over her and bicker about how to care for her. Mrs. Walker cooked and cleaned, and AJ did the rest.

One day, Jasmine was awakened by many smells from her kitchen. Mrs. Walker baked many cakes, pies, and pastries of Beast Dump and Dragon Bamboo.

"Mom!", AJ exclaimed. "She's a tiger, not a cow! How many stomachs do you think she has? How do you expect her to eat all of this?"

"I'm feeding her cold.', Mrs. Walker retorted.

"It seems like you're feeding the neighborhood.", AJ stated.

Even the girls helped and kept Jasmine in high spirits. It wasn't long before Jasmine recovered, and AJ's daughters ate what Jasmine couldn't finish off their grandmother's cooking.

"I'm sorry, Jasmine. She always overdid it with me when I was sick as well.", AJ said, embarrassed after his mother left.

"I really didn't mind, AJ," Jasmine insisted with a smile.

CHAPTER 5

THE ROAR HEARD AROUND THE BLOCK

One Saturday morning, Christie, Joan, and Lily played with some animals on the block. They were animals from school: three wolf pups named Starlight, Stormy, and Sunlight, and their fox pup friend named Max. They played hockey, wolves versus raccoons, with Max as the goalie. That's when JoJo came with his son, Mo, along with Randall and five other badgers, two of Mo's age and the remaining three, JoJo's age. Lily ran to get her father, AJ, while Christie hid behind Starlight. Jasmine saw all the commotion from her window and was outside just as one of the little badgers pushed Sunlight and laughed.

"That's enough!" Jasmine roared. Her roar alerted the entire neighborhood, and everyone watched from their windows.

Mo glared at her, turned to his father, JoJo, and asked, "Dad, why is a tiger interfering with our fun?"

Jasmine squatted down and stared at Mo with tense, gold eyes. "Does it look like these animals are having fun?"

Mo swallowed and quickly backed away and hid behind JoJo. Lily returned with AJ and said, "Dad, those three badgers, Mo, Keith, and Fletch, are the ones that bully Christie at school."

"Your daughter is scum, just like you," JoJo hissed at AJ. JoJo's friends and their sons shouted in agreement.

Jasmine growled deeply, and the badgers and hawk backed away in fear. "You will listen because I'll tell you this, and it will be the last time. This is my neighborhood, and these are my neighbors. You will answer me if you or your children continue to come after them. JoJo, you will tell your son to leave Christie alone, and you will leave AJ and his family and every family in this neighborhood alone.", she growled.

Suddenly, a police car drove over, and the officer was a fox. "Max, what's going on?" he asked.

"Daddy, these badgers are bullying my friends," Max said.

The officer glared at JoJo and said, "Joseph Christopher Sterling, why are you harassing animals five blocks from your street? And I have gotten complaints from other neighborhoods. Report to the station tomorrow at 8 AM. Don't leave the house for the rest of the day until then."

The officer drove away, and when he was gone, the whole neighborhood laughed except for Jasmine, AJ, and his girls, whose jaws had dropped.

"Joseph Christopher Sterling?" said a she-wolf. "I didn't think he was a 'Joseph.'" said a hyena.

JoJo slouched his shoulders to appear smaller, embarrassed. He wouldn't even look at his friends who were chuckling and failing to hide it. Mo and his friends mouthed 'I'm sorry' to Christie, her sisters, and their wolf friends before JoJo stormed away, leading his friends and son with him.

"Be quiet! JoJo's name isn't funny, and we shouldn't laugh. Sure, he laughed, mocked, and abused you for who you are for a long time, but that doesn't mean we do the same thing to him. We treat others like we want to be treated. I'm quite sure he was bullied for his name, which is why he prefers to be called JoJo, so show respect, and we call him JoJo", Jasmine roared.

The neighborhood grew silent as JoJo turned to Jasmine and nodded in respect. JoJo was on house arrest, and his son and his friends were suspended for a week. The bullying stopped, and Christie was looking forward to going to school. Because of what Jasmine did, more animals came forth with the information she could use for her book; even stubborn and wary animals were convinced to share their stories. Max and his father, Officer Arthur Swiftred, wanted to share their side. They could express that they didn't like how some animals were treated, revealing that Jasmine wasn't the only one who felt that way.

With the latest information, Jasmine was busy trying to organize everything, and she asked AJ to help so it would come out smoothly and together nicely. AJ still had work but always supported and checked up on Jasmine. When AJ had to work overtime, Jasmine had his daughters spend the night at her place, and they, too, helped her with the book while she helped them with homework. Jasmine felt supported and loved, and she wondered why her family didn't support her like that in her dream and passion for writing. She thought maybe it was because they couldn't see what she saw and didn't understand, and at times, Jasmine wanted to call them, but she would talk herself out of it, thinking they wouldn't listen.

CHAPTER 6

EYE OF THE TIGER

After gathering all the info and writing nine drafts, Jasmine finished the book and had it titled "Lost and Forgotten." Jasmine wasn't artistic and knew pictures would give the reader the power it needed for animals to understand the struggle. Her first thought was AJ.

"You could pay any artist you want for providing pics for your book, you know," AJ stated.

Jasmine stood up straight, looked the raccoon in the eye, and said, "That may be true, but I choose you. Your art reflects everything I've written; I wouldn't have gotten all of it without you. Please, AJ? I will acknowledge you for your work and ensure you get credit."

Christie tribute and suggested what to take photos of that Jasmine and AJ didn't think about. After a few more conversations, Jasmine convinced AJ to be the illustrator and photographer of the book. Jasmine made the deadline and turned in her work. The book company that gave her six months and extended the due date when Jasmine asked looked it over, and after a week, when the publishers finished reading from cover to cover, they denied the book, the main reason that AJ was the one who provided the photos and art for the book.

That, however, didn't stop Jasmine or AJ. Other book companies denied the book, too, for the same reason, and some tried to convince Jasmine to find another artist, but Jasmine refused. Only one book publishing company agreed to publish the book. Amazingly, the company was controlled by a human named Joshua Davis. He was on board with having the book out to the public. At first, only humans and lower-class animals read the book. Then, a lion named Clifford bought and read the book and decided to meet Jasmine. He told her he loved her writing and wanted to sponsor her. They even went out to dinner to discuss it. "I'll do it if the deal includes my partner, AJ," Jasmine stated. Clifford dropped the deal, for he feared the embarrassment of having a raccoon in it. That broke Jasmine's heart, but she stuck to her morals. The duo returned to AJ's home, and after AJ had dinner with everyone and sent his girls to bed, he sat Jasmine down to talk.

"Jasmine, I love you as a friend, and I'm grateful you don't treat me like the others do. You don't look down on me or act superior to me, but I wonder why you are so invested in the cause. Why are you fighting so hard for me and others like me?" AJ asked.

Jasmine took a deep breath and said, "Because we are all animals, no one is more or less important than the other. We all need to love, support and appreciate each other. Back at my home in Dragon Bamboo, my family pressed me to become a doctor because of my interest in animals and how different our features are. My family is a family of doctors, and even I claimed I wanted to do it, but along the way, I felt stretched, stressed, and out of place, and I only felt like myself when I wrote a short tale."

"I decided to be a writer.", Jasmine continued. "My family claimed I was going through a phase and that it would pass, and I would return to Medical School. I had to show them I was serious, so I switched my study choice, and then I moved here because no one seemed to be listening. The system labels us even though not everyone fits the label given. I'm a writer and a tiger who loves all life, and you are a raccoon who is an artist, who loves his daughters, supports them in whatever they want, and dreams of being, and I refuse to leave you behind because of what I am."

After Jasmine stopped talking, AJ hugged her and whispered, "Thank you." That's when Jasmine's cell rang. It was Clifford, and he told her he had been thinking and realized that he liked Jasmine more than his reputation and was willing to put it on the line to support what she offered. He revealed that he wanted to be friends with other animals besides those he shared with the upper class. Clifford revealed that he was once friends with a wolf and a raccoon, but his other friends and parents harassed him verbally until he broke ties with his raccoon friend and wolf friend. He secretly still resents his inner circle for that.

"I understand, Clifford. I really do.", Jasmine stated warmly.

After an hour's phone conversation, a deal was made, and it included AJ. The book "Lost and Forgotten" became the #1 best-seller globally, but that was not why Jasmine was happy. What did make her happy was that those who read the book tried to do better for the raccoons and others mistreated. Even JoJo and his son, Mo, were kinder. However, Randall, the hawk, refused to change and was arrested for going after a bat family. Jasmine, Clifford, and AJ even toured worldwide for book signings. During the tour, AJ saw Jasmine's family, who were proud of her and what she had accomplished. After Jasmine and her family had a good long talk and cleared the air, Jasmine had a stronger bond with her family. AJ's daughters, Christie, Joan, and Lily, also joined the tour, and they enjoyed seeing new places and trying new things.

When Jasmine and AJ weren't promoting the book and were finally home, they had 'Family Day,' which is when they do an event with their friends and family. On May 4th, Jasmine's friends and parents joined Jasmine, AJ, his daughters, JoJo, Mo, and Clifford, with his friends at the movie theaters to watch a Star Wars movie marathon.

Everyone was dressed as a character, but Jasmine stole the show by dressing up as Ahsoka Tano. Clifford dressed as Chewbacca, Lan was Leia Organa, AJ was Luke Skywalker, JoJo was R-2 D-2, and Mo was BB-8.

Everyone enjoyed watching the classic films but enjoyed each other's company more. They were the only animals dressed as Star Wars characters, while other animals wore Star Wars shirts, so they were frequently asked to pose for pictures. Human Star Wars fans also asked them; most had the same idea of dressing as the characters. Two hundred ten women alone were dressed as Princess Leia, and they fawned over Lan.

After the movies, there were reenactments and lightsaber duels outside the theater. Then, at midnight, Officer Arthur, as a stormtrooper, drove by, telling everyone to go home. Clifford made a Wookiee roar, and Arthur responded, saying, "Rebel Scum," which made everyone laugh while they disbanded and went home. Later at noon the next day, Jasmine, AJ, and his girls watched from their windows as the Cinco de Mayo parade marched down the street. Christie, Joan, and Lily were entranced by the colors red, white, and green and the aroma of the food. It reminded Jasmine of the Lunar New Year celebrations back in Dragon Bamboo.

Of course, the parade was cleaned up, but the joyful vibes still hung in the air. Jasmine prepared to unwind and relax for the night; however, AJ and his girls wanted to have fun. Jasmine smiled as she listened to AJ and his daughters play games and music at the lowest volume until she fell asleep. Jasmine was happy that this neighborhood had become a home for everyone and that she could give that to AJ, Christie, Joan, and Lily, and she hoped for more to come for them and even her.

CHAPTER 7

ANIMALS MAKE THE WORLD GO ROUND

"Lost and Forgotten" was such a big hit that Jasmine and AJ were demanded to do another book tour. However, everyone seemed to enjoy visiting Jasmine's parents and family and getting to know her more. During the book signing tour, AJ, Jasmine, and AJ's girls did much more. They saw new lands, climbed mountains, explored oceans, met other animals, and learned new cultures. They learned to cook the cuisine, played games, and explored the vast garden of Jasmine's childhood home. The lotus pond AJ learned was Jasmine's favorite place in the garden.

Jasmine shared with AJ and his daughters about the times she would come to the pond. She went there to think, study, and even draw and paint when inspired. She led them into her old room to show all the flowers' drawings and paintings of the garden. One flower that kept popping up was a white lotus flower. AJ figured that this flower had sentimental value to Jasmine, and he felt that the flower would be brought up soon.

During the trip, Christie took it upon herself to record everything they did through photos and notes. When they returned home, Jasmine and AJ worked on their next book, "The Places of the World, Then and Now." Christie shared credit as the author of the book. The pictures of Jasmine's family garden and many animals living there were used for the book, "The Places of the World, Then and Now," and Jasmine's family expressed which pictures were their favorite.

Thanks to the first book, "Lost and Forgotten," the change began slowly, but raccoons and the other animals that made up the Lower Class in Beast Dump could have better jobs and lived in better places. Many businesses hired AJ for designs, most of which were from companies he constructed buildings for. AJ used the money to upgrade and improve his neighborhood and afford schooling that supported his daughters' interests. Christie got into a Fine Arts school and studied Art and Creative Writing. Joan decided to explore being an engineer, and Lily wanted to be a pilot.

Jasmine continued to write and continued to use AJ for pictures. Jasmine and AJ would invite friends from AJ's block to be guest speakers and performers during new book introduction gatherings. One of the popular ones was a wolf named Midnight, the father of Starlight, Stormy, and Sunlight; the wolf pups and the MC who performs optimistic songs that he wrote himself. Midnight's music was used when "Lost and Forgotten" became a documentary.

Midnight became a close friend to Jasmine and AJ because Jasmine, by making the book, helped him and his daughters, and AJ's daughters, Christie, Joan, and Lily, were good friends with Starlight, Stormy, and Sunlight. They were able to hang out a lot more.

Jasmine and Clifford decided only to be friends and professional business partners. Clifford reconnected with the raccoon and wolf he was friends with long ago and cleared the air with his family. AJ's girls still see Jasmine as their mother, even after she met and married a handsome tiger named Matthew Daniels.

Before the marriage, Christie, Joan, and Lily were very protective of Jasmine and were initially skeptical toward Matthew. They even voiced to Jasmine that they were afraid that they would lose her. However, after Jasmine and AJ explained that even though she loves Matthew, it didn't mean she doesn't love them any less, and he came around them often, they bonded with him and called him 'Uncle Mat.' He was a marine and now works as an officer as Arthur Swiftred's partner. Matthew found peace with Jasmine, her family, and her friends, and when he had episodes of post-dramatic stress, everyone was there for him and comforted him through it. Everyone knew it never went away, but it got better. Matthew even began a Tiger Chi center, where he taught

wrestling, boxing, and Martial Arts. Mo and Max were the bright pupils there. During a black belt ceremony, the students wanted to see their teacher battle Jasmine and her friend, Sue, who came to visit. Everyone was surprised and amused when the tigresses both beat Matthew.

Jasmine was happy to have married Matthew and believed that AJ should have the joy of loving someone like that. She convinced AJ to find someone and told him she'd put him on a dating site if he didn't start doing it himself. He was initially stubborn, especially since he still missed his girls' mother, but then he met a Gym Instructor named Rebecca. She was mild, shy, and delightful. Christie, Joan, and Lily expressed that they wanted her as their mother, and Jasmine was excited since she knew Rebecca from her gym. Jasmine loved attending Rebecca's classes and would bring Rebecca during visits at AJ's so she could get to know the girls more. AJ had to tell his daughters and Jasmine to calm down and let the relationship between him and Rebecca come naturally. AJ was very impressed when Matthew had Rebecca as his first adult student in his classes at his center.

Rebecca understood that AJ still missed Marsha, and she proved to him and his girls that she knew she would never replace her. Mrs. Walker adored her and was less restrained in saying AJ should marry Rebecca. AJ tried to tell his mother the same thing he said to his girls and Jasmine, but Mrs. Walker didn't listen and hinted at his proposing to her. She even pampered Rebecca just like she indulged Jasmine when she was sick.

When AJ finally did propose to Rebecca, Jasmine, and her family, AJ's and Rebecca's families were proactive with the wedding plans. AJ was the happiest he had ever been and was grateful to have found love in Rebecca, pride and joy with his daughters, peace with his mother, and a friend in Jasmine, and he was glad he became her friend.

One afternoon, Jasmine and AJ spent the day together, just walking around the neighborhood, sharing stories about their lives, even though they already knew each other since they lived next to each other and had breakfast, lunch, and dinner as friends. During dinner, Jasmine asked, "I never asked what 'AJ' stood for. Can you tell me?"

AJ began to squirm, and he looked away, embarrassed.

"It stands for Adam James.", he muttered.

Jasmine cocked her head at him. "Adam James?"

"Yes. My full name is Adam James Steven Walker", AJ confirmed. He was waiting to hear her laugh but saw her waiting with a patient smile.

"I like your name. What's wrong with it?" she asked.

AJ sighed with a light puff and explained. "On my mom's side, James is the family name. On my dad's, however, it's Adam. When Mom was married into the Walker Family, and I was close to being born, the families argued about what name I should have if I were born a boy. My parents decided that I would bear both names to keep the peace. I hated it growing up, especially when certain family members would say my full first name every time they talked to me or when aunts called me by my full name when I did something wrong, which is why I tell people to call me AJ. It's shorter and easier, plus at least JoJo's name is simple. Joseph seems way better than Adam James."

Jasmine laughed this time, but not cruelly and loudly; it was bubbly and sympathetic. "I quote Juliet from Shakespeare's Romeo and Juliet, 'What's in a name?'. Your name is noble, and you are a very noble raccoon. Sure, we all may have questioned why our parents give us names, especially when we are younger and don't understand. Over time, we learn that it's not what people call you; it's what we answer to, and we have answered to our names since we first acknowledged them.", she stated.

She added, "Plus, names passed on in the family have history and stronger meaning. When people say our names and think about our memories, it brings joy and comfort because they get to know the soul who had that name. Our names become part of who we are, not the other way around, and when our time on Earth ends, we leave every mortal and physical thing behind, including our names. Your daughters will take pride when talking about their father, Adam James."

AJ sighed and smiled. "It seems you always know what to say. Thanks for that. I'll sign my full name from now on, but I still want to be called AJ." he informed. Jasmine and AJ laughed at the statement and resumed to another topic.

As time passed, Jasmine thought about how proud and happy she was to have helped the animals at Beast Dump, especially the raccoons, AJ, and his daughters, to whom she was neighbors and friends to. They were happy to have her around, and they seemed complete with Rebecca being in their family. Even after Jasmine started a family with Matthew, she ensured everyone she cared about was included in everything she did. Jasmine also provided that in everything she wrote and published, the lesson of love was there, for all living things always need love. Jasmine also hoped that as life went on, she expected to teach that same lesson to her cubs.

THE END